For Martha – J.D.
For Marco – N.S.

First published 2009 by Macmillan Children's Books
a division of Macmillan Publishers Limited
20 New Wharf Road, London N1 9RR
Basingstoke and Oxford
Associated companies throughout the world
www.panmacmillan.com

ISBN: 978-1-4050-8943-2

Printed in Belgium by Proost

Toddle Waddle

Written by
Julia Donaldson

Illustrated by
Nick Sharratt

MACMILLAN CHILDREN'S BOOKS

Toddle

waddle.

Flip flop,

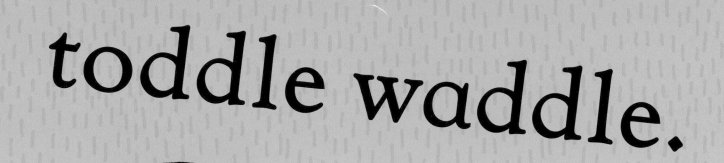

toddle waddle.

toddle waddle.

Clip clop,

hurry scurry,

flip flop, toddle waddle.

Ting-a-ling, clip clop,

hurry scurry,　flip flop,　toddle waddle.

Leap creep,

ting-a-ling,

clip clop,

toddle waddle.

hurry scurry,

flip flop,

Stop!

Boing boing, splish splash, puff puff,
roly-poly, crunch munch, slurp slurp,

chitter chatter, helter-skelter,
see-saw, snip snap, ping pong.

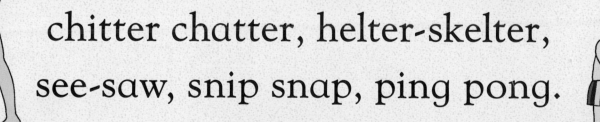

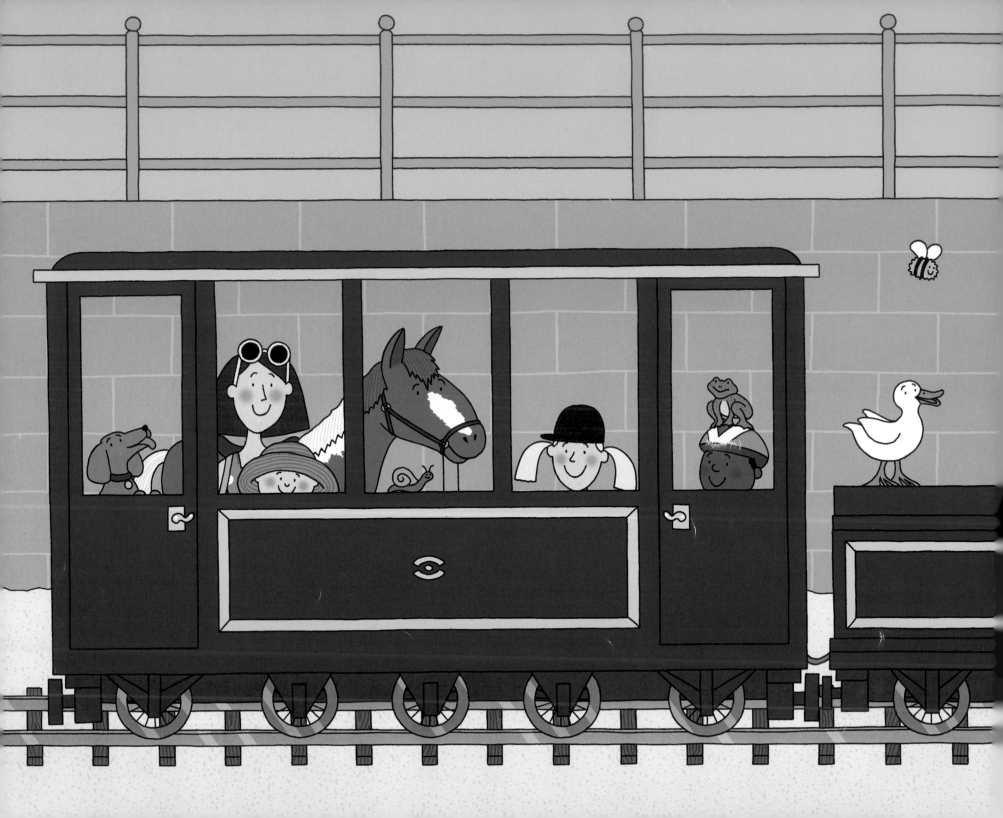

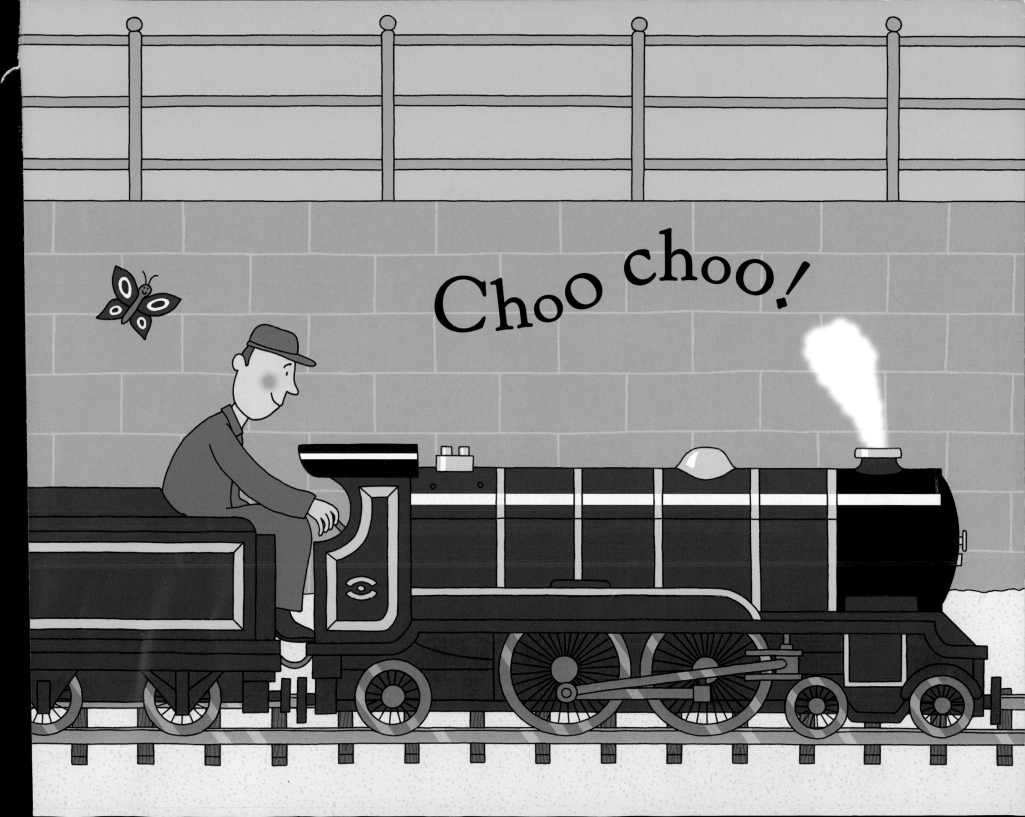

Flitter flutter, buzz buzz, leap creep, ting-a-ling, clip clop,

hurry scurry, flip flop, toddle waddle.

Bye-bye!